For Raquel, Maria and
Llanos x P.M.

For the original Alfie
McPoonst, the best dog
ever. With all my love
forever x D.McN.

First published 2020 by Walker Books Ltd
87 Vauxhall Walk, London SE11 5HJ

10 9 8 7 6 5 4 3 2 1

Text © 2020 Dawn McNiff  Illustrations © 2020 Patricia Metola

The right of Dawn McNiff and Patricia Metola to be identified as author and
illustrator of this work has been asserted by them in accordance with the
Copyright, Designs and Patents Act 1988

This book has been typeset in Personal Manifesto and Filosofia

Printed in China

British Library Cataloguing in Publication Data: a catalogue record for this
book is available from the British Library

ISBN 978-1-4063-6991-5

www.walker.co.uk

**WALKER BOOKS**
AND SUBSIDIARIES
LONDON · BOSTON · SYDNEY · AUCKLAND

# Love From
# Alfie McPoonst
## The Best Dog Ever

Dawn McNiff

illustrated by

**Patricia Metola**

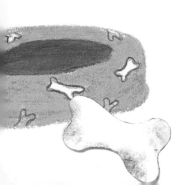

To Izzy
The Dog Bed
The Lounge
Izzy's House
Near the Little Park

From: Alfie McPoonst
The Nicest Cloud
Dog Heaven
The Sky

Dear Izzy,

I'm a Sky Dog now.
I live in Dog Heaven,
because I died.

I miss you lots, but it's BRILLIANT here. There are hundreds of parks, thousands of sticks, and a million-trillion dog sweets.

No cats bully me. I get to scare big wolves and chase postmen. I never need to have a bath. (There are no poodle parlours in Dog Heaven.) And the big dogs LOVE my good-boy-shake-a-paw-trick!

Love from,
Alfie McPoonst x

PS I still miss you loads though.

Dear Izzy,

I get ALL my favourite treats here.

There are actual burger bars and
ice-cream vans for dogs. And
I'm allowed to eat cowpats.

Love from,
AMcPx

Dear Izzy,

Did I tell you I've got loads of Sky Dog mates?

We play tug-of-war with our teddies.
We go for walks by ourselves – nude,
without our collars or leads! We do roly-polies
in flowerbeds, squash all the flowers and
NO ONE shouts.

And we're allowed to snooze on sofas,
chew shoes, wee up slides and poo on lawns.
It's so fun.

Love from,
AMcPx

Dear Izzy,

I miss our huggles and tummy-tickles.

But the BEST part of Dog Heaven is that
I get to snuggle with my dog-mum again
at bedtime.

Love from,
AMcPx

Dear Izzy,

I watch you through a star peep-hole every day. It makes my tail very waggy. Please wave.

Love from,
AMcPx

PS I left some dog fluff behind the sofa.

Alfie McPoonst
The Best Dog Ever
The Nicest Cloud
Dog Heaven
The Sky

Dear Alfie,

Thank you for my fluff.
I keep it in a special heart
locket, so I'll never forget
you, even when I'm 100.

Love from,
Izzy xx

PS I love you forever.